Josephine's Pouch

Written by Geneva Witmer
Illustrations by Vianney Hwang

Stay true to
you!

♡ - Geneva

Dedication

For anyone who has ever felt like they had to change who they are to feel accepted

Acknowledgments

I would like to acknowledge people in my life who have supported me. My dad is the inspiration for the dad in this story. Like his character, he has continually provided me wisdom and encouragement. My mom is someone who helps keep me focused with my creative goals and never allows me to grow lazy when it comes to developing my strengths. I am grateful for my little sister, Capri, who chimes in with the funniest comments and brings joy to my life. When I was little, my grandma would tell me the best bedtime stories which made me want to be a good storyteller like her. Thank you to the illustrator, Vianney Hwang, whose artwork made my visions come to life in such a vibrant way. Thank you, Bill Foley, for applying your professional photography skills to prepare for publishing. My time and externship with Girls Inc. of Orange County helped me put into words things that had been stirring in my heart. I want to thank my friend, Trevor Welsh, for sharing his love of photography and talent with me and providing me with my author's photo. Lauren Vargas took the first few drafts of this story and provided great feedback, which turned my goal of writing a book into a reality. I want to thank Kristin Heathcoat, Traci Kennedy, Terri Kelley, Tracey Mayebo, Jaxon Mayebo, Lexie Mayebo, Heidi Bazansky, Paige Bazansky, Heather Miller, and my freshman English teacher, Mrs. Holmes, for taking the time to read my story and assist with revisions and editing. My list of acknowledgments would not be complete without mentioning my sophomore and junior year English teachers Ms. Helmer and Mr. Peace. They care about their students in a manner that extends far beyond assignments or grades, and their constant care for me has been a blessing in my life.

Balboa Press books may be ordered through booksellers or by contacting:

Balboa Press
A Division of Hay House
1663 Liberty Drive
Bloomington, IN 47403
www.balboapress.com
1 (877) 407-4847

This is a work of fiction. All of the characters, names, incidents, organizations, and dialogue in this novel are either the products of the author's imagination or are used fictitiously.

ISBN: 978-1-9822-0076-3 (sc)
ISBN: 978-1-9822-0077-0 (e)

Library of Congress Control Number: 2018903465

Print information available on the last page.

Balboa Press rev. date: 03/29/2018

BALBOA
PRESS
A DIVISION OF HAY HOUSE

"Mom! Dad! I cannot be late for my first day of school!" Josephine exclaimed.

"Just a second, sweetie. I have to get my video camera," her dad eagerly replied as he finished upstairs.

"Do not forget about me!" her mom shouted excitedly as she busily stuffed her laptop into her pouch and files into her briefcase.

Josephine was starting her first day of kangaroo class. She had been dreaming of this day and was eager for school to begin. She shoved her colored pencils, pink highlighters, markers, papers, and lunchbox into her pouch. Josephine was ready!

Her parents and younger brother Joe hopped down the stairs into the living room where Josephine patiently waited. "Are all of your supplies for this first day of school in your pouch?" her mom calmly asked.

Josephine responded with gusto, "Yes, Mom. I have everything I need." Josephine leaped outside, followed by her family.

The school was only a block away, which was perfect hopping distance. Josephine's dad followed behind his three family members with his trusted video camera. This was surely a day he wanted to remember.

"If you need anything, remember that your teacher will help you… got it?" her mom checked. Josephine nodded her head and continued bouncing down the block where she curiously noticed a tiny, green stem growing between two cracks along the sidewalk. Absentmindedly, she wondered if this could be the beginning of a beautifully bright, beaming flower.

Finally, they arrived at the school and gathered next to the classroom. Josephine's eyes and smile grew big as she saw many other kangaroos her age springing through the doorway of the class, forming a small mob. Whispering goodbye, she hugged her mom, dad, and brother.

"Have a great first day, Josephine. I will miss you," her teary-eyed dad whispered back as he kissed the top of her furry head. Josephine told her parents goodbye one last time and confidently hopped into the classroom with her shoulders back and head held high.

The teacher, Mrs. Coco, greeted all the students as they entered the classroom. She directed them to sit on the oversized, grassy rug in the center of the room. Josephine made her way to the rug and sat next to a few chatty boys.

Mrs. Coco jumped to the front of the room near the board and gleefully announced, "Welcome to kangaroo class! I am delighted that you are all here. We are starting this year with a drawing contest. Please draw something that is meaningful or important to you. Can everyone please take out a piece of paper and colored pencils?"

Josephine reached into her pouch and dug for her supplies. She heard a laugh coming from a boy to her left, "Hehehehe-hahahaha. You don't have a backpack. All the boys in our class have cool, new backpacks. See?"

Another boy's voice chimed in, "Girls just have pouches. Backpacks are for cool kangaroos only." Until now, Josephine had never thought anything different or negative about her pouch. Embarrassed and confused, she took a big kangaroo breath and listened to her teacher's drawing instructions.

Gripping a colored pencil in her left forepaw, she brainstormed ideas for her drawing. Josephine got a bright idea. She would draw the tiny green stem growing between two cracks in the sidewalk that she observed on her way to school that morning. She used her imagination to draw what the flower would look like when it blossomed. When Josephine looked over her shoulder, she saw the boys near her drawing baseballs, sports cars, and video game logos. Since it was so different from the others, Josephine wondered if her drawing would be acceptable.

As she colored, she also could not stop thinking about the remarks the boys had made about her pouch. After working for nineteen minutes, Mrs. Coco rang her bell and declared, "It is time for snack. Please turn in your picture, and I will excuse you to go outside and eat."

Josephine hopped to the front of the room and handed her welcoming teacher her abstract artwork. With a smile beaming from ear to ear, Mrs. Coco proclaimed, "Wow! I have never seen a picture like this. I am looking forward to discovering more about your creativity and all the big ideas in your brain, Josephine."

After thanking her teacher, Josephine leaped through the classroom door and headed out to eat. She sat at an empty, round table near beautiful oak trees. Suddenly, a group of five rowdy boys from her class bounced over to the table where she quietly sat. The table was now full of hungry kangaroos. Josephine watched the boys take their snacks out of their bulky backpacks. She timidly slid her petite lunchbox out of her pouch and began to eat her tender leaves and fresh flowers.

Boomer, the boy sitting directly across from her yelled, "Hey! No pouches allowed at this table. Backpacks only." The other boys at the table copied Boomer and nodded their heads in agreement.

"What is wrong with a pouch?" Josephine questioned.

Boomer answered, "Pouches are strange. Backpacks are for those who are smart. If you have a backpack, you will get a great job someday. Everyone knows that."

Josephine's eyes filled with tears, and she trudged over to the tiny table where the girl kangaroos were chatting. A storm of emotions crashed down on her. She looked down at her pouch, humiliated, and realized there must be some hidden rules about who she could fit in with. The last thing she wanted was a pouch; she wanted a backpack like the boys. Boomer's words echoed in her thoughts, and she worried for her future so intensely that she barely noticed the bell signaling the end of snack.

As the students gathered in the area of the classroom marked 'Scholar's Pocket', Mrs. Coco read aloud from her favorite book. The main character in the book faced many challenges but always found a way to overcome them. Josephine knew the lesson in the story was important. However, she could not stay focused because a brilliant idea was bubbling up in her brain. She could not wait to get home.

Mrs. Coco rang the bell. The first day of kangaroo class was finished. Josephine frantically rushed out the door. When she arrived at home, she cruised into the garage, straight to the place where her parents kept boxes containing special items from when *they* were kids. Josephine searched through her dad's old boxes. Diamonds of joy sparkled in her blue eyes when she discovered the item she'd been looking for. There it was. Her dad's old, rugged backpack from when he attended school. The backpack, colored in dark shades of gray, was large in size. She planned to transfer her supplies into the backpack and wear it to school the next day, so all the boys would think she was smart, not strange. Josephine hauled the backpack upstairs and hid it in her vibrant closet full of colorful bows that she enjoyed wearing. In Josephine's world, life simply felt better accessorized with a bow.

That night, Josephine could barely sleep. She could not get her mind to stop obsessively dreaming about how incredible she would look at school using a backpack, instead of her pouch. She envisioned jacks, jills, and joeys dropping their jaws in admiration as she entered the classroom.

Since she did not want her parents to notice that she was using her dad's old backpack, she set her alarm clock extra early. When she heard her parents waking, she flew downstairs with an extra spring in her step. Swiftly, she moved all her supplies into her dad's old backpack and swung it over her shoulders. Yikes! She realized this was going to be a heavy load on her shoulders.

"Bye, Mom. Bye, Dad. Bye Joe! I am going to hop to school by myself today," Josephine shouted, while leaping out the front door. Due to the backpack, she struggled to hop as quickly as she had on the first day.

A small feeling of disappointment consumed her heart when she once again passed the green stem growing between the sidewalk cracks. Would it ever grow into the gorgeous flower that she envisioned for her class drawing contest?

As she stood in the messy line in front of her classroom, she saw Boomer and his friends. Josephine decided to hop over to them and eagerly declared, "Look at my backpack! See! I am smart, too! Pouches are *so* strange."

Boomer rolled his eyes, "Are you serious? You clearly don't understand the rules because backpacks are for boys *only.* Girls can never have a backpack." Boomer's followers nodded their heads in agreement, and they mockingly laughed at Josephine's backpack.

Josephine's cheeks grew rosy red with embarrassment. Holding back tears, she hopped away from school without permission and hurried for her house. Although she wondered if she may be breaking a major school rule, she let her emotions lead the way. This situation required an honest chat with her dad, who was known for giving loving advice.

Barely noticing the green stem in the cracks of the sidewalk, she almost crushed it with the intensity of her hops. *Knock. Knock.* Her nervous hands hit her front door. With shocked eyes, her dad opened the door and noticed the tears trickling down her face like raindrops descending from a leaf after a rainstorm. Then, he saw his old backpack slumped over her shoulders.

"Honey," he calmly spoke. "Why are you wearing my old backpack? You have an exquisite pouch to use."

Before answering her father, Josephine stormed inside the house and threw the hefty backpack across the living room floor. Josephine's voice cracked, "I wanted to prove to some of the boys at school that I was smart like them. They told me yesterday that backpacks are for smart kangaroos, but today they told me that backpacks are only for boys. I don't know what to do."

"Josephine. A backpack or pouch does not define intelligence. You have nothing to prove to any boy. You have a mind that is smart, and you are able to accomplish anything you set out to do," her father shared.

"If I don't have a backpack, then how will I fit in with Boomer and his friends?" Josephine inquired with honest concern.

"Sweetie, you do not have to look, act, talk, or agree with any boy or any other kangaroo to earn respect. Continue to think for yourself, embrace your pouch, and be bold."

Josephine replied, "I understand what you are saying, but my pouch still feels strange."

"Strange? Your pouch is not strange. It is absolutely lovely! Your pouch is an advantage because one day you can carry a baby roo in your pouch and still have a wonderful job at the same time. Your pouch is actually quite a unique gift," Josephine's father expressed.

A wide smile formed on Josephine's face before wrapping her arms around her father for an enormous kangaroo hug. She was beginning to recognize that her differences made her special, not strange.

With a better understanding of herself, Josephine was determined to skip back to school with a newfound joy for how she was wonderfully created. The desire to carry a backpack was gone, and she felt ready to stand up to anyone who told her otherwise.

Cruising down the sidewalk with her father by her side, something caught her attention. Stunning pink petals were forming on the green stem that sprouted between the cracks in the sidewalk. Josephine picked the fresh, fragrant flower and carefully placed it in her pouch.

As she approached school, she discovered it was the final recess time. She proudly bounded over to a group of students and noticed her classmate, Mira, had a frown on her face.

"Mira! Are you alright?" Josephine asked.

With a shaky voice, Mira responded, "Boomer and his friends told me that my sparkly, purple bow was strange."

Josephine took the opportunity to speak the truth to Mira. "Strange? Your bow is not strange. It is absolutely lovely! It is a reflection of your sparkly personality and fits you perfectly. You do not have to look, act, talk, or agree with any boy or any other kangaroo to earn respect. Continue to think for yourself, embrace your bow, and be bold!"

These words were comforting, and Mira's frown was immediately wiped from her face. Josephine glanced over her shoulder and noticed a group of other kangaroos had also heard her empowering words. They also had smiles on their faces. Josephine had put many of their own thoughts and feelings about fitting in with others into words.

The bell rang for the students to go back to class. Once everyone was in class and seated on the grass rug, Mrs. Coco excitedly said, "I would like to announce the winner of our drawing contest."

"It is obvious that I am going to win," Boomer mumbled across the classroom.

Mrs. Coco pulled the winning portrait from the pile on her desk and announced, "The winner of the contest is Josephine!" Mrs. Coco held up Josephine's picture of a giant pink flower for all her classmates to view. Everyone put their paws together and applauded, except for Boomer, who stared down at the floor in distress.

Instead of soaking up the glory, Josephine decided that she needed to be a kind kangaroo. She lovingly went over to Boomer and gently tapped him on his shoulder. Boomer gazed at Josephine and seemed shocked to see her. Josephine reached inside her pouch, pulled out the pink flower, and placed it in Boomer's paw. "Thanks," Boomer softly replied and set the flower in the top pocket of his backpack.

Now Josephine knew exactly who she was and how she was uniquely created. She felt confident in her own intelligence and proud of her differences. **Josephine is a bright, pink flower with a one-of-a-kind pouch.**